The Flying Bear

Written By:

Edwin Torres

I'd want to dedicate this book to my older brother, Xavy. You were someone who had no boundaries and pursued any goal you set for yourself. This was the source of my story's inspiration.

XT, I adore you.

This is the story of a flying bear.

Noah was a famous flying bear. Everyone in town knew Noah; he spent every day in the air. He was flying from north to south and east to west. All you saw was Noah's plane flying around.

Noah loves his plane. When he wasn't flying, he was working on his plane. Noah spent his time cleaning it, painting it, and fixing it up. Noah was the first and only flying bear in town. Most of the pilots were birds. There was no one like Noah.

OIL

Noah wasn't always a flying bear. Noah was like the other bears. Noah played, worked, ate and slept a lot. Bears weren't known for flying. Ever since Noah was a child, he has always had a love for airplanes and aviation. He collected airplanes, and his room had airplane posters all over it. Noah told everyone that he wanted to fly, but all of his friends made fun of him and told him that it would never happen.

TOY BOX

Noah's friends scoffed at his idea of flying; no one saw it possible since there was no flying bear. His friends told him to leave that for the birds. Noah loved the idea of flying. He dreamed of being next to the clouds looking down on everyone. Noah always had a toy plane at school. Sometimes, he got sad and started to think that maybe everyone was right; I cannot fly.

One day, Noah woke up sad and realized that his love of flying would never come true. Everyone told him it was impossible. His mom saw that he was unhappy. He explained why he was sad. His mom told him they were right. There was no flying bear. She also told him that doesn't mean it's impossible. His mom explained that you need to work hard for your dreams when you love something so much. Don't give up until your dreams come true.

Noah realized that he needed to work harder for his dream. His friends continued to tease him as he grew older, but he wouldn't listen to them. He enrolled in flight school and did not get in right away. He wasn't happy, but that didn't discourage him. He didn't want to give up on his dream.

FLYING
SCHOOL

After a lot of hard work, Noah made it to flying school. He was happy and willing to work hard. His friends couldn't believe it. Noah was closer to making his dream come true. The news that Noah went to flight school spread through the city. The young bears began to see other bears around town playing with toy airplanes.

Noah started learning to fly his plane at school. He wasn't the best of all. The rest of the students were like birds. They were better than him. Noah was frustrated at times. He could see that he was not good at flying. Noah told his mom how he felt and his mom said he wasn't a bird; flying would not come naturally. He would have to work harder to be good. Noah realized that he needed to work harder even on days when there was no school.

In the end, he made it! He graduated from flying school. He was the top of his class! All his friends who made fun of him at some point were there supporting him and apologizing. Noah received many awards because he was good at flying. Noah was the first flying bear. His mom was proud of him. Many years after graduation, there were many bears enrolled in flight school.

The lesson of the story is to never give up on your dreams. The path will never be easy, but with hard work, anyone can achieve all dreams.

The End